For all of our Beans,
Who we love the most.
Those still here with us,
Who we hold so close.

Those who we have lost...
Oh, We miss so dear.
Such wondrous ways,
Which they reappear.

Floating in our souls,
On wing or on feather.
In every rainbow,
Together Forever.

-soul & sweetD

Beezly Publishing
First published in the United States

Publisher's Cataloging-in-Publication data
Adventures In BeanTown™ / A soul & sweetD Creation; by soul; illustrated by sweetD
ISBN 978-1-7334613-5-1 (Hardcover)
LCCN 2019913073

Adventures In BeanTown & ♥ TM by soulEnterprises, LLC
Copyright © 2018 by soulEnterprises, LLC
2683 Via De La Valle G611
Del Mar, CA 92014

Artwork created with watercolor & ink
Printed in China

Counting Down...
10 9 8 7 6 5 4 3 2 1
Blast OFF

Adventures In BeanTown

XO ♡

A soul & sweetD Creation

Beezly Publishing
An Imprint of soulEnterprises, LLC
™

Gazing down from afar on a lovely town,
a town with the friendliest beings around.

These beings aren't human though, as you can see.
These beings are Beans, all sorts and sizes they be.
These beings who are Beans have traveled the world
from where they have been,
all gathered together to build this town
that they now peacefully live in.

What kinds of Beans live in BeanTown, you may ask?
One day we shall meet them all, from the first to the last.
But a more serious issue in our town of Beans has been planted.
It's now time for the Legend of the BeanTown Bandit!

This day was just as others,
as all of our Beans carried on.
Then a being, who was not a Bean,
our BeanTown he stumbled upon.
This being was not a Bean,
but rather this being was a mole.
A mammal living underground,
and burrowing through his holes.

What's this?
What's this great scent that I've found?
It smells good...
Good enough for me to pop up
out of the ground!

It was rare that this mole was ever even seen,
as his journeys to the surface were few and far between.
But it just so happened that on this particular day,
stumbling across our town of Beans
is where the Bandit found his way.

You see, the Bandit was quite interested
in our happy BeanTown.
Not as a guest,
but because these Beans
smelled like the best food around.

He smelled his way here,
since he could not see.
For he was a mole,
and moles cannot see.

WANTED

- DESTRUCTION OF FARMLANDS
- SCAVENGING SPROUTS
- EMBEEZLEMENT
- BURROWING UNDER TOWN LINES

Our Beans had never before
seen the Bandit around.
They'd only heard of the other
pillaged towns that were found.

So when the U.S. Navy Beans laid their eyes on the Bandit coming close,
they sounded our town's alarm and locked down at their posts.

They tried to protect all the others,
but they were scared it was too late.
For he had broken through the barbed wire,
and dug under the front gate!

The alarm was now sounding,
and our Beans became frantic.
They had no idea the Bandit
would be so quick and gigantic.

With no time for plans,
and no way to defend,
they all grew fearful
that this was their end.

But as the Bandit began to bring his reign down,
our Beans joined together to help defend BeanTown.
Each Bean searched deep within to muster up the courage
and assembled in the town's court to deliver their message.

Sheriff B.B.Q. on his Painted Pony Bean
was the first one to speak,
while the rest stood terrified behind him,
their Bean knees trembling and weak.

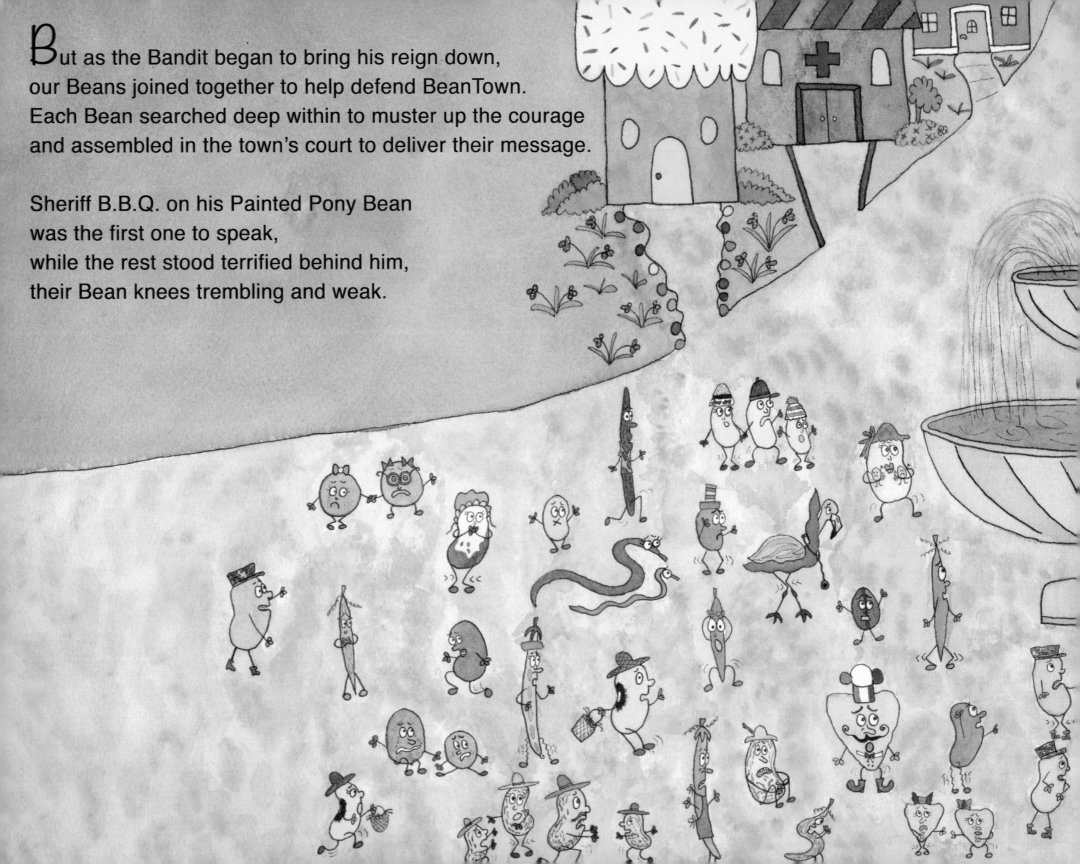

"I came because I'm starving,
and without eating you that's how I'll stay!"

Then Banzo stepped forward,
"Ciao Signore Bandito, Potrei Suggerire!
Instead of eating us, I can provide you an amazing Italian meal
in exchange for leaving us safe in BeanTown...
Do we have ourselves a deal?"
The Bandit scarfed down Banzo's meatballs and spaghetti.
However, it was going to take far more than that
for him to leave this town be.

"This food is most scrumptious, I really must say!
But it's dessert I now crave, so get out of my way!"

"Ia ora na!"
Tanoa's voice rang out like a scream.
"Will you please let me serve you
my vanilla ice cream?"

The Bandit snatched the dessert
without a bit of hesitation.
What had started as mayhem
was settling to a calmer mediation.

Calm enough that the Japanese Edamame stood his Karate Beans down,

as a fight with the Bandit was the last thing any Bean wanted in BeanTown.

The Bandit's belly was so happy
his gear no longer fit.
Thankfully, our town's tailor came through
with a custom design he knit.

Once the Bandit got all dressed up
in his fancy new attire,
he noticed he had been cut
from crawling under the barbed wire.

"No problem!"
called out the Pink Flamingo Bean vet,
who stitched up the Bandit
like she would for any other pet.

"Ahhhh, that feels much better,"
the relieved Bandit sighed.
By calming him down,
our Beans allowed their own fears to subside.

They all joined back together
after sharing their unique abilities.
Their sole request to the Bandit remained,

**"Can you leave our town
safe and happy now, please?"**

Each Bean held their breath
in fear of what would happen next,
while the Bandit stood thinking,
as he was a bit perplexed.
You see, he had pillaged town after town
for all of his existence.
Yet he never stopped long enough
to make a better difference.

The Bandit realized that all these Beans
were generous and brave,
and this is how our BeanTown
came to be saved.
Our Beans were able to teach the Bandit
their valuable lessons,
with each one taking pride
in whatever they were best in.

It became clear to the Bandit that...

A Bean is a Bean,
No matter their color.
To the Bandit who can't see them,
No one is different from the other.

A Bean is a Bean,
Through the thick and the thin.
A Bean is a Bean,
Traveled the world from where they have been.

A Bean is a Bean,
Each sound unique when they talk.
A Bean is a Bean,
Assorted journeys of life they all walk.
A Bean is a Bean,
Dark, light, tall, or small...

By putting aside these differences,
they saved themselves
from the Bandit,
and joined one for all.

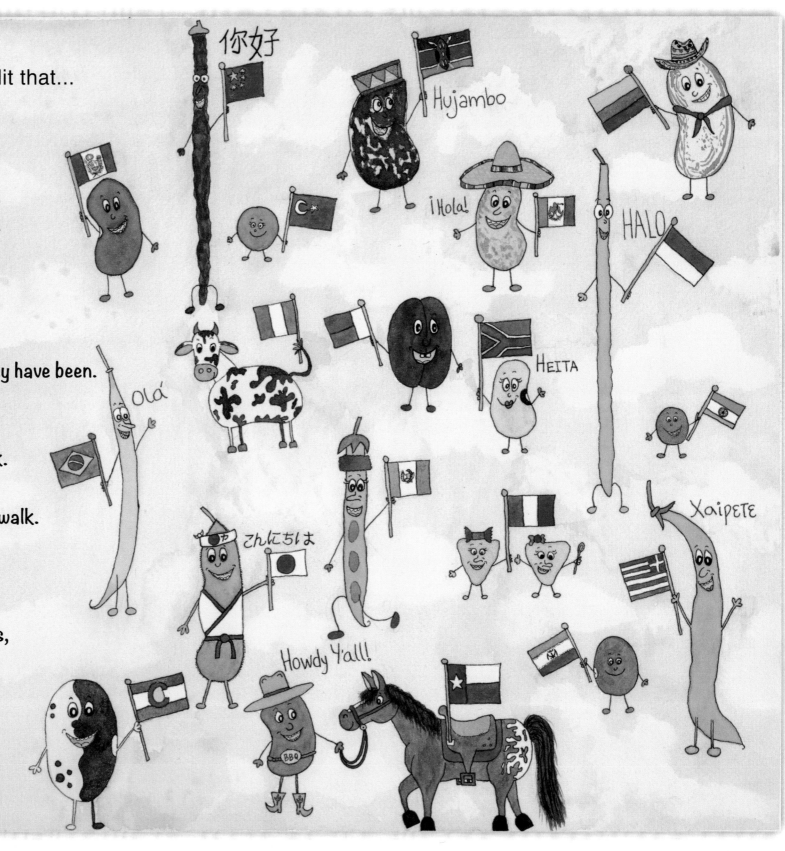

This glorious turn of events called for la grande celebración,
so Pinto and his familia threw the biggest fiesta they have ever thrown!

The Dutch Common Bean joined in to play a special mix he had saved for a gig just like this,
as this was one party that no Bean in BeanTown could afford to miss.
Our Beans and the Bandit enjoyed this most epic night,
and seeing their amazing time together was quite a splendid sight!

When morning came,
all of our Beans saw the Bandit off on his new journey.
Although his journeys from here on out
will be different as different can be.
The Bandit still can't see,
but has now been taught to understand.
That instead of pillaging our wonderful BeanTown,
They can all live together hand in hand.

So now...
When we gaze down from afar on this lovely town,
our town with the friendliest beings around.
We still see all these Beans as different,
because different is good.
But more importantly we see them as one,
because seeing them as one
is just the way we should.